CAJUN COLUMBUS

CAJUN COLUMBUS

Text by
ALICE DURIO

Illustrated by
JAMES RICE

Based on characters created by
DAVID DURIO

PELICAN PUBLISHING COMPANY
GRETNA 1975

Library of Congress Cataloging in Publication Data

Durio, Alice.
  Cajun Columbus.   46549

    SUMMARY: Relates how the Cajun Pierre Las-
trapes discovered Spain and in turn helped Columbus
discover America.
    [1. Columbus, Christopher—Fiction]
I. Rice, James, 1934-II. Title.
PZ7.D9342Caj   [Fic]   75-20484
ISBN 0-88289-074-3

Manufactured in the United States of America

Published by Pelican Publishing Company, Inc.
630 Burmaster Street, Gretna, Louisiana 70053

Designed by Gerald Bower

CAJUN COLUMBUS

Once upon a times w'en peoples don't got much educate, an' dey don't got telly-vision an' feetsball an' bessball to cass an eye on, dere was a poor fella w'at dey call Pierre Lastrapes, him.

Now dis Pierre some smaht mans, I 'ope to tole you.

Dass 'cause he resamble his great couzan Pere Hebert (pronounce a-bear) w'at got his parish church down in Pont Breaux where all dem peoples pass a good time, eat dem *ecrevisse*[1] an' make de *fais do do*.[2]

---

[1]*crawfish*
[2]*big dance*

Mais, ennyhow, dat fella done somet'ing good w'at mos' nobody knew anyt'ing about. Dass how come I got to tole all you peoples de tale of Pierre's great great explorin' wit' de worl' back in de days w'en peoples was pickin' on dem pirate instead o' pickin' dem pepper fo' Ferdinand an' Isabella.

Well, Pierre got good favor wit' de devil, an' of cou'se he like to pass pla-zure wit' dat blackberry wine—de stuff mamon Tee-Ta make him. An' Pierre would got his enjoys an' *laissez de bon temps rouler*[3] planty time. He special like to pass a good time wit' his frien' dem Viking w'at come from de odder side de big h'Atlantic Bayou, w'at dem peoples w'at don't know no better call de h'Atlantic h'Ocean. Wit' dem Viking, Pierre, him, would make music on his windbox an' damon-strate dat Cajun twice-step.

---

[3]*let the good times roll*

One day Pierre, I garontee you, got hisse'f carried away. An' carried away for a fack. He mos' drowned hisse'f wit' his mamon's good drinkin' stuff. Yeah, an' he dance an' play his windbox 'til his arms an' legs can't go no more. An' wit' dat he lay down hisse'f in his pirogue an' commenced floating away across de big h'Atlantic Bayou. A big wind pushed Pierre's pirogue way far away.

W'en Pierre finally open his eye good, he didn't racognize anyt'ing w'at he saw dere. One t'ing for sho', he was close by some lan', an' a man on de sho' was spoke to him like dis: "*Comment ca vas,* ma' good frien', how y'all makin' out?" Pierre make so sopprise he don't say nothin', an dat mans wit' de front name o' Christopher an' de behin' name o' Columbus say: "Where you brought you'se'f from, an' where you got you'se'f a pirogue like dat, hanh?"

Pierre say: "Mais, you mean to tole me you don't know Pierre Lastrapes? An' furdermo' an' on de side, dis pirogue is de vary bes' you can find aroun' Pont Breaux."

Ole Chris reflec' hisse'f wit' astonish, an' den he say: "Ma' frien', you mean to tole me you jus' drif' you'se'f from de odder side o' de worl', you? Why, das de same iden'ical t'ing I been tole-in' peoples, but dey don't pay me no never mind. Of cou'se I know better—dat de worl' is roun' like one dem tennis ball dey gonna invention a coupla hunnert years from now. So tole me, Pierre, how you did dat, an' how you pass a good time on you' side o' de worl'."

Pierre t'ought about dat summore, an' he say wit' sheepish all over his face: "Me, I sho' don't recomember nuttin' good about how I brought ma'se'f here. An' dass a fack."

Columbus say: "Well, tole me dis. Do you t'ink iss possibles fo' de worl' to be roun' like one dem tennis ball we talk about?"

Pierre say: "W'at you t'ink, you? But fo' sho' de worl' is a-roun' jus' as positive as me an' you is sittin' here makin' some spoke."

Columbus say: "What I'm axin' you is do you t'ink de worl' is presactly shape like a ball, or like one dem a-lip-tickal t'ing?"

Pierre say: "Mais, you didn't know de worl' is shape like a great big *boudin*[4] wit' a bite missin' where you can fall you'se'f in dem boilin' hot water an' burn like a red crawfish in a stewpot?"

Columbus say: "How you like dat! Me, I never heard dat how-you-call t'eory befo'. But tole me, ma' frien', since you brought you'se'f all de way from de odder side de worl' an' h'especial over de h'Atlantic h'Ocean, w'at you call de h'Atlantic Bayou, would you like to be one dem navigator fo' de Spaniel king an' queen, dem?"

_____

[4]*sausage*

Pierre say: "De Spaniel king an' queen? Where dey at?"

Columbus say: "Dey residence deyse'f in dis country which is call Spain, it."

Pierre pass himse'f some axcite, I 'ope to tole you. "Manh," he say, "dis is de place dose Viking tole me dey come close, close, close to befo' dey come make sociable wit' me to pass pla-zure. Mais, sho' enuf I'll be you' navi-alligator. An' I garontee you I can navi-alligate to de odder side de h'Atlantic Bayou faster den a grease hog can slide down a bayou bank."

Columbus say like dis: "Pierre, you got you'se'f a deal. Me, I got t'ree de bigges' pirogue in de worl' to sail off across dem h'ocean—de Niña, de Pinta, an' de Santa Maria."

An' Pierre, his eye shinin' wit' joyful, say: "Well, less got goin' an' r'at now. I need ma'se'f a navi-alligator hat an' one dem once-eyed spyin' glass w'at you got dere."

W'en averyt'ing was shapeship, Pierre an' Columbus an' his crew brought deyse'fs in dem big pirogue an' make sail fo' de voyage across de h'Atlantic Bayou. An' Ferdinand an' Isabella, de Spaniel king an' queen, came down to de pirogue to see dem off, an' de queen wave her sepulchre an' dey bot' wave deyse'f back. An' she say: "Took good care o' youse'f, you year? *Au 'voir.*" (In Spaniel country dey usual say *hasta la vista* or *adios,* but in Cajun story averybody spoke dat good Anglish or Franch).

Avery day Pierre would got his once-eyed spyin' glass an' cass an eye on dat sun on de h'Atlantic Bayou. An' one day dey got a storm come up wit' a big sudden, an' dose poor pirogue was swimmin' an' swaying' wit' dem h'angry water somet'ing pat'etic. An', worse of all, dat navi-alligator Pierre los' his bearin' plumb, even wit' dat once-eyed spyin' glass w'at he got dere. He don't know where dey at, an' he so confuse he don't know where dey even come from, an' dass bad!

All dem mens on de t'ree pirogue—de Niña, de Pinta, an' de Santa Maria—pass deyse'fs some tarrify, I 'ope to tole you. Dey suspec' fo' sho' dey gone fall off dat missin' bit o' de *boudin* an' got deyse'fs boil like dem red crawfish. An' furdermo' an' on de side, Pierre pass some lonesome t'ought about his heartsweet Clotille, w'at he got a big infection for.

Pierre kept tryin' to find dat sun wit' his once-eyed spyin' glass, an' it pass a long time dey been in dat h'Atlantic Bayou wit' mos' not a t'ing dey can did about dat. De h'Atlantic Bayou was heavin' somet'ing fierce, an' likewise de sailin' mens.

Den one day when averybody was sick to dey stomach, dat Pierre cass an eye t'rough dat once-eyed spyin' glass an' his heart leap up like a gar after a mosquito hawk when he saw a big white bird—w'at dey call a pelican—an' w'at had in his beak some white mag-a-nolia.

Pierre start to shout: "I tole you, I tole you! See, Columbus, dat pelican got in his beak some mag-a-nolia, dass flower from dat mag-a-nolia tree. Dat brought me to de conclude dere mus' be some land aroun' here."

Den dat Pierre look again in his once-eyed spyin' glass an' he saw de lan'. Pierre shouted: "De lan'! Doggone, it's de lan'!"

An' sho' nuf dey got some lan' out dere on de 'rizon. An' mo' happier den a houn' dorg wit' a juicy soupbone, Pierre start to play his windbox. An' de mens was so delirimous wit' glad dat dey dance enuf to make dem pirogue rock, you year?

W'en dey brought deyse'fs to sho', Columbus sat his foots on dat groun' an' he poke a flag in de soil to claim it fo' dem Spaniel ruler Ferdinand an' Isabella, dem.

Now all dat celebratin' make Columbus an' his men intoximous, an' soon dey fas' asleep. Dat was de firs' good *do do* dey got since dey wave goodby to de Spaniel king an' queen. But jus' while dey snooze deyse'fs dere some red mens—dem Attakapas Indians—w'at hunt in dem wood brought deyse'fs out. Columbus jump to his feets, but his knee buckle dere an' one dem red mens catch him. So Columbus shout to Pierre to brought hisse'f r'at now an' lickety split, an' sho' enuf Pierre come a-runnin' out de wood where he been explorin'.

When dem red mens took a good look at Pierre wit' his navi-alligator hat an' once-eyed spyin' glass dey fall deyse'fs on dey knee 'cause he look like one dem sun god. Dey tole Pierre wit' sign lang-wich dey tie up Columbus 'cause dey t'ought he was gonna took dey lan', an' furdermo' an' on de side, dey know dat flag ain't no peace flag, it. But averyt'ing brought isse'f all right in de wash 'cause dey so impress wit' Pierre.

Columbus an' his crew was save, an' dey pipe de peace smoke wit' de red mens. Plus dem Spaniel got claim on de lan' beyon' de giant *boudin*. An' since averybody help to fin' it, dey make decide to call it Avery Island.

Boy, dat make Columbus mens happy like crazy. An' on top o' dat, de Spaniel king an' queen would pass plazure to know dis Avery Island got some red hot pepper, even mo' better den w'at dey got in de Spaniel king country. So now averybody could make dat good *boudin*.

So Columbus brought hisse'f back to Spain to tole de good news to Ferdinand an' Isabella, dem. An' dem Indian show Pierre how to plant hisse'f some pepper, an' Pierre show dem how to pass a good time an' eat dem *boudin*.

An' Pierre, him, stay at Avery Island, an' befo' you can say Jacques Robichaux, he got hisse'f a wife an' chirren w'at he call Ti-Beau, Ti-Belle, Ti-Jean, and Ti-Pierre.

Yeah, he done good fo' hisse'f dere. Mais, poor
fella, wit' all his adventure wit' Columbus to got to
Avery Island, he never got hisse'f de credit fo'
findin' dat wonderful lan' beyon' de giant *boudin*.